18:40

A Winter
Concert

To Terry, Kent, and Mone with Love ✉

Library of Congress Cataloging-in-Publication Data
Takao, Yuko
[Fuyu no hi no konsato. English]
A winter concert/by Yuko Takao.
p.   cm.
Summary: The mice in the audience at a piano concert enjoy the
music and carry it home with them as it continues to bring joy to
their world.
ISBN 0-7613-0301-4 (lib. bdg.)
[1.Music—Fiction. 2.Concerts—Fiction. 3. Mice—Fiction.] I.Title.
PZ7. T1635Win   1997
[E]—dc21   97-1425   CIP   AC

First published in Japan by Cacoo-sha Col, Ltd., Tokyo
as Fuyu No Hi No Konsato by Yuko Takao
First published in the United States in 1997 by The Millbrook Press, Inc.
2 Old New Milford Road, Brookfield, CT 06804

A Winter Concert

by Yuko Takao

The Millbrook Press   Brookfield, Connecticut

One snowy afternoon,

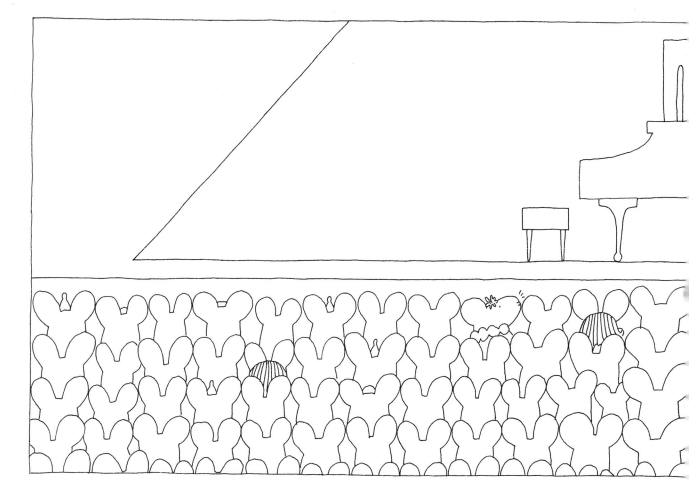

The audience gathered.

she went to a concert.

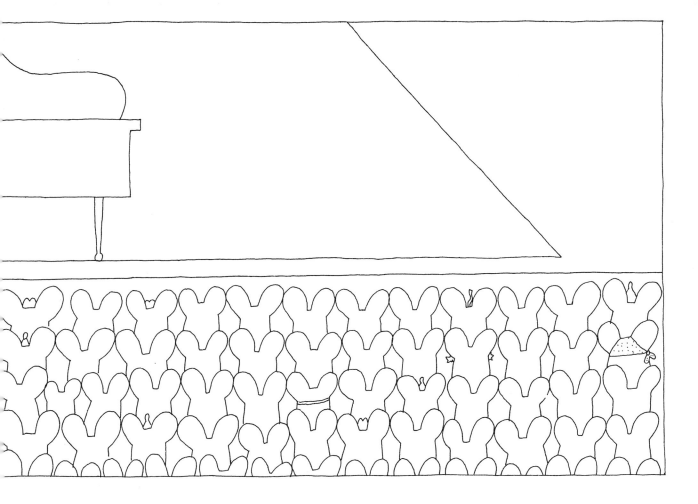

The pianist

began to play.

He made music,

Ta-dum, ta-da…

Beautiful, beautiful music…

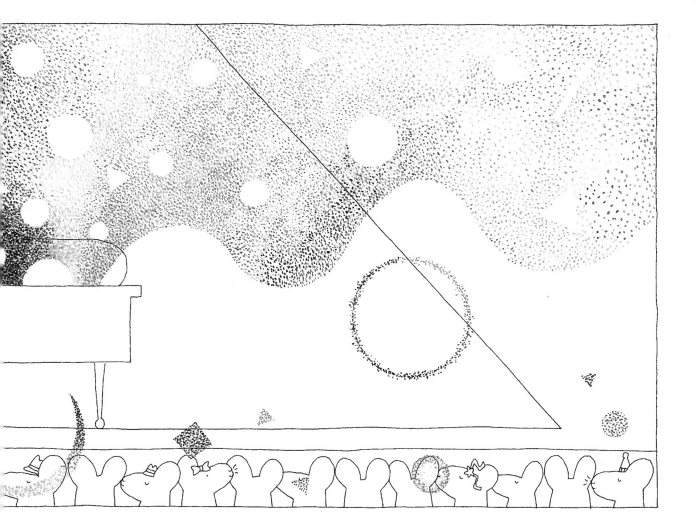

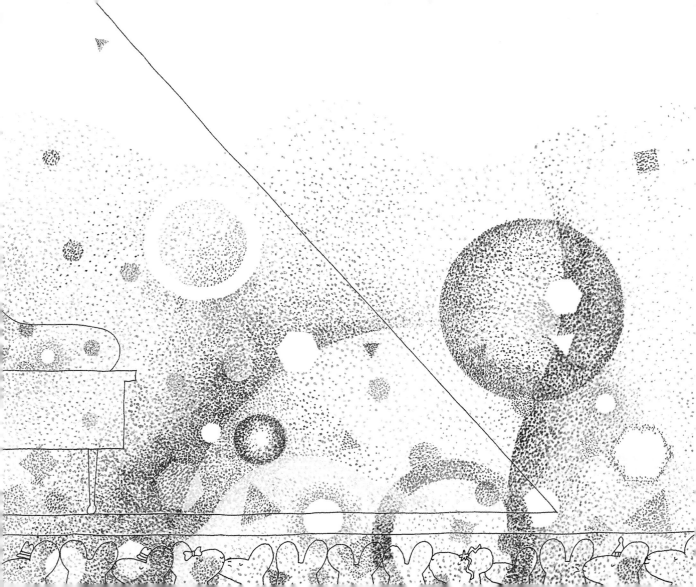

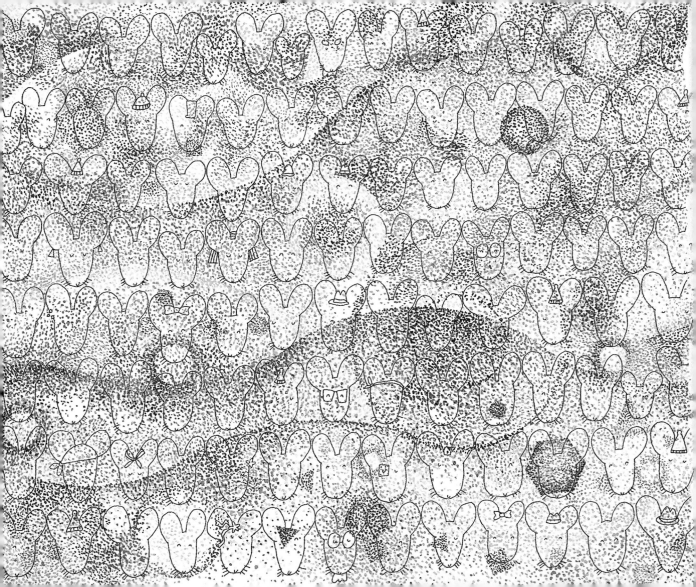

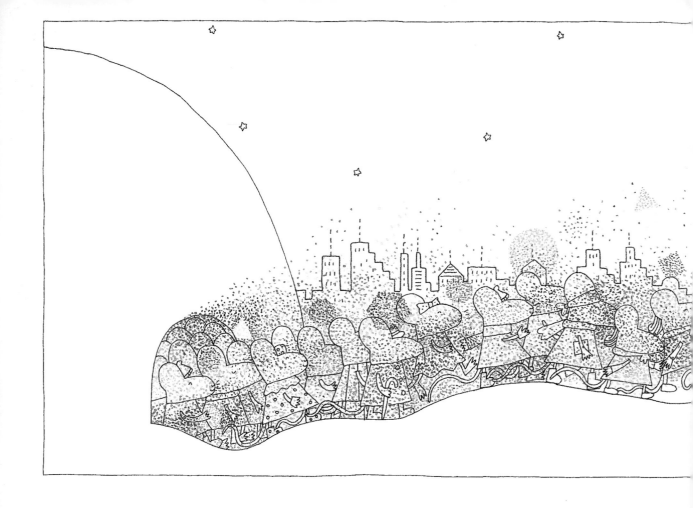

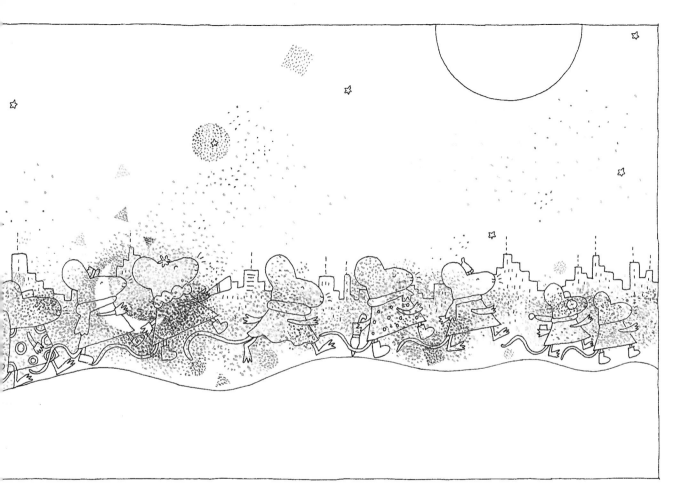

The concert ended but the music did not.

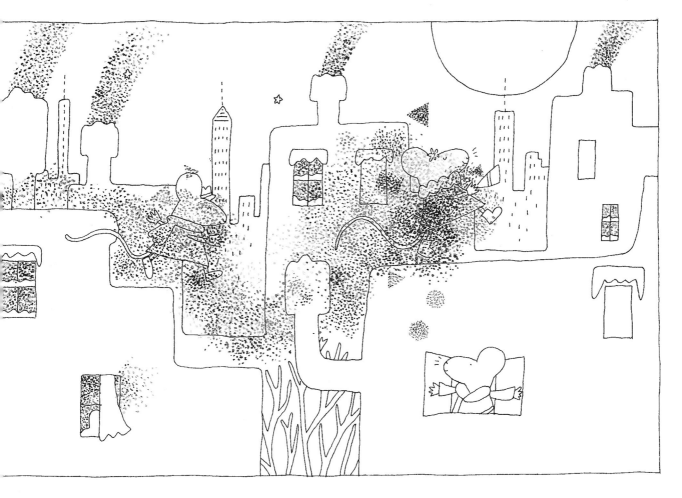

It paved their pathways home.

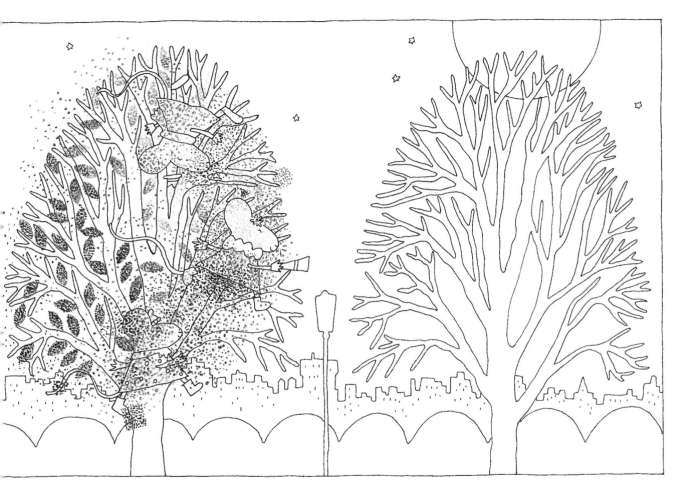

It colored their world.

The music made the wintry night magical.

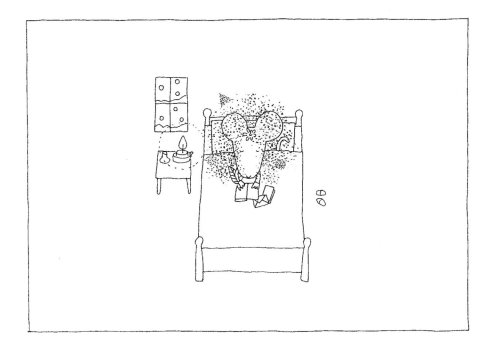

She shared the music with her diary.
She wrote a letter.

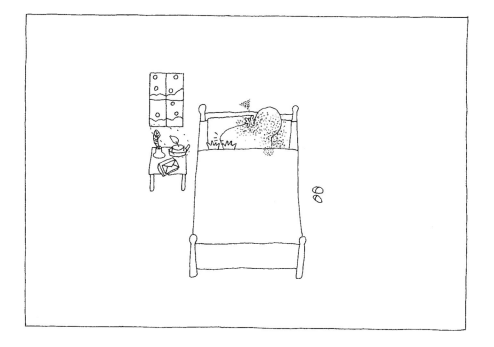

Ta-dum...ta-da...

Good night.